HE-MAN
AND THE MASTERS OF THE UNIVERSE™

THE SWORD OF GRAYSKULL

Adapted by Shelby Curran

He-Man and the Masters of the Universe
developed for television by Rob David

Based on the teleplay by Bryan Q. Miller

SCHOLASTIC INC.

ISBN 978-1-338-81929-8

10 9 8 7 6 5 4 3 2 1   22 23 24 25 26

Printed in the U.S.A.   40

First printing 2022

Book design by Jeff Shake

In the center of the universe is the planet of Eternia.

Eternos is the capital city and home of the Royal Palace.

King Randor watches the magical city from the glittering towers.

It is quiet. But never trust the shadows!

Teela, a street-witch, sneaks into the palace to steal the Sword of Power.

As Teela touches the sword, there is a flash of gold light!

She hears a mysterious voice in her head.

"Sword. Past. Secrets. Power . . ."
the voice whispers. "Masters of the Universe!"
Then, it is quiet. The sword is glowing.
Teela is surprised!

Teela hears the Royal Guard coming.
She needs to escape with the sword.
   "Get her now!" the guards yell, chasing
after Teela.

Bwoop-bwoop!
A skysled is passing by.
Teela jumps on!
She speeds away, holding the sword tightly.

Kronis is an evil inventor and a warrior.

Evelyn is a wicked mystic and a witch.

"Teela hasn't failed us yet. She will find what we seek," says Evelyn.

"With that sword, the Power of Grayskull will soon be ours!"

As Teela shoots down from the sky, she remembers the mysterious voice.

It tells her that the sword does not belong to Evelyn.

"Bring the sword to the champion!" the voice calls. But who could that be?

Adam is a young boy raised in the jungle by the Tiger Tribe.

He has no memory of his life before being adopted by an old cat named Cringer.

Could he be the lost royal prince?

Adam climbs down a cliff to rescue Kitty, a talking tiger cub.

Kitty is stuck on a tree limb.

He climbs on Adam's shoulders.

When Kitty spots a dragonfly, he pounces.

Adam and Kitty slide down the cliff!

"Adam, are you two done yet?" asks Krass, Adam's friend from the Tiger Tribe.

"Or do you wanna hang out some more?" She helps Adam and Kitty to safety.

Adam is thankful that Krass was there to make sure he and Kitty were all right.

Krass tells them that Cringer, Kitty's uncle, is missing after going hunting.

They must save him—to the rescue!

Cringer is captured by robots that cage and hurt animals.

"Release me, or incur the wrath of my tribe," calls Cringer.

Adam and Krass swing through the treetops to Cringer's cage.

"I knew you'd come for me!"

The cage won't open! The bots are trying to stop them, but Adam has an idea.

"You up for a game of ram-ball?" he asks.

Adam flings Krass up into the air, where Krass points her grappling gun down at the ship and fires. The grapple line then pulls Krass helmet-first into the ship, smashing the controls!

"Goal!" yells Krass.

The cage falls off the line into the jungle.

The dust clears and the bots are defeated.
When the cage opens, Cringer is free!
"Tiger Tribe for the win!" shouts Krass.
Adam walks over to them for a group hug.
"Tiger Tribe forever!"

The friends walk back to the Tiger Tribe village.

Even though Cringer does not have claws, he still went hunting to help the tribe.

Krass thinks Adam should get a special stripes tattoo to prove he is part of the Tiger Tribe.

"Every lost soul the tribe adopts gets their stripes when they so choose. Adam isn't ready." Cringer says.

Adam still wears the gold cuff he's worn since he was lost.

The cuff is all Adam has from his old life, and he does not want to get rid of it.

Krass is worried that Adam will leave the tribe one day.

Suddenly, Teela falls from a tree.
Adam tries to catch her, but she uses her
magic to float in the air.

"Can we help you, Tree Lady?" asks Adam.

Teela explains that a voice in her head
told her to come here.
    The Tiger Tribe villagers do not like magic.
They capture Teela!

"Why aren't you afraid of magic like the rest of your people?" asks Teela.

"To be clear, the cats don't like magic," says Adam.

Teela tells Adam he sounds like he is from the city.

"Just count your lucky stars you're out here," she says. "No one likes the King."

Teela tells Adam that the voice in her head sent her to bring a package to the champion.

"Being a champion is about defending those who can't defend themselves," says Adam.

They are both surprised.

Evelyn and Kronis finally arrive at the Tiger Tribe village with an army of bots.

"We'll find the girl and the sword," says Evelyn.

She turns to Duncan, an apprentice of the evil team.

"Duncan, have the robots burn the village."

"I can't do that!" says Duncan.

He doesn't want to hurt anyone in the village.

"Coward," Kronis says, grabbing the remote from Duncan.

He will take control of the bots instead.

Teela hands Adam the package
with the sword.
    She tells him to run far away and hide
it while she creates a distraction.
    The village burns in the distance.

"My voice and I will come back for it," says Teela to Adam.
He is their only hope!

Cringer helps to fight the bots but is cornered. Before he can be attacked, Duncan smashes the bot!

"Thank you, Kind Stranger!" says Cringer.

"Ahhh, talking tiger!" yells Duncan, in surprise.

The bots chase Teela through the jungle.
Evelyn spots Teela!
"There she is, get her!" calls Evelyn.
Evelyn hits her with blasts of dark magic.

Sensing that Teela is in trouble, Adam comes back to help her.

"Get the real sword out of here!" orders Teela.

"I had a sword this whole time?!" asks Adam, shocked.

"Hand it over, thief," calls Evelyn, getting closer.

But suddenly, the cuff on Adam's wrist connects to the sword.

The sword glows as light swirls around him.

Adam reads the words circling the sword: "By the Power of Grayskull . . . I have the power?" The gold energy from the sword becomes a vortex of power.

Lightning crackles! The others watch as Adam is transformed.

"He's . . . a man," admires Krass.

"The Power of Grayskull," says Teela in awe.

Adam is He-Man!